Mic

Play It By Ear

by Kristin Smedley
illustrated by Kim Crothers

PICTURE WINDOW BOOKS
a capstone imprint

Words to Know

blind—not being able to see with your eyes

Braille—a system of writing where the letters are represented by raised dots that can be felt to read

cane—a tool used to help someone walk independently; some visually impaired people use a white cane

master—to become skilled at

memorize—to learn something by heart so you can remember it without looking it up

recital—a show where people sing or play an instrument

Published by Picture Window Books, an imprint of Capstone
1710 Roe Crest Drive, North Mankato, Minnesota 56003
capstonepub.com

Copyright © 2026 by Capstone. All rights reserved. No part of this publication may be reproduced in whole or in part, or stored in a retrieval system, or transmitted in any form or by any means, electronic, mechanical, photocopying, recording, or otherwise, without written permission of the publisher.

Library of Congress Cataloging-in-Publication Data is available
on the Library of Congress website
ISBN: 9780756588816 (hardcover)
ISBN: 9780756588991 (paperback)
ISBN: 9780756588854 (ebook PDF)

Designed by Jaime Willems

An ebook edition with audio narration is available. Visit capstonepub.com/librarians/ebooks for more information.

Printed and bound in China. 6274

TABLE OF CONTENTS

Chapter 1
Meeting Mr. Foster 8

Chapter 2
Wrong Notes 13

Chapter 3
The Recital 20

Meet Michael

Michael loves music. He sings and plays piano. He also loves playing and watching sports. Baseball is his favorite. He loves being outside too.

Michael is blind. He does not see with his eyes. He uses his tools of blindness to do all the things he wants to do.

Michael uses a white cane to confidently walk on his own. He uses glasses to see bits of light and shapes more clearly. He wears sunglasses outside. He uses Braille to read.

Braille

Braille is a series of dots that make up letters and words. Look at each letter and the dot pattern that goes with it.

In a Braille book, every dot is raised so you can feel it. Then you can read with your fingers.

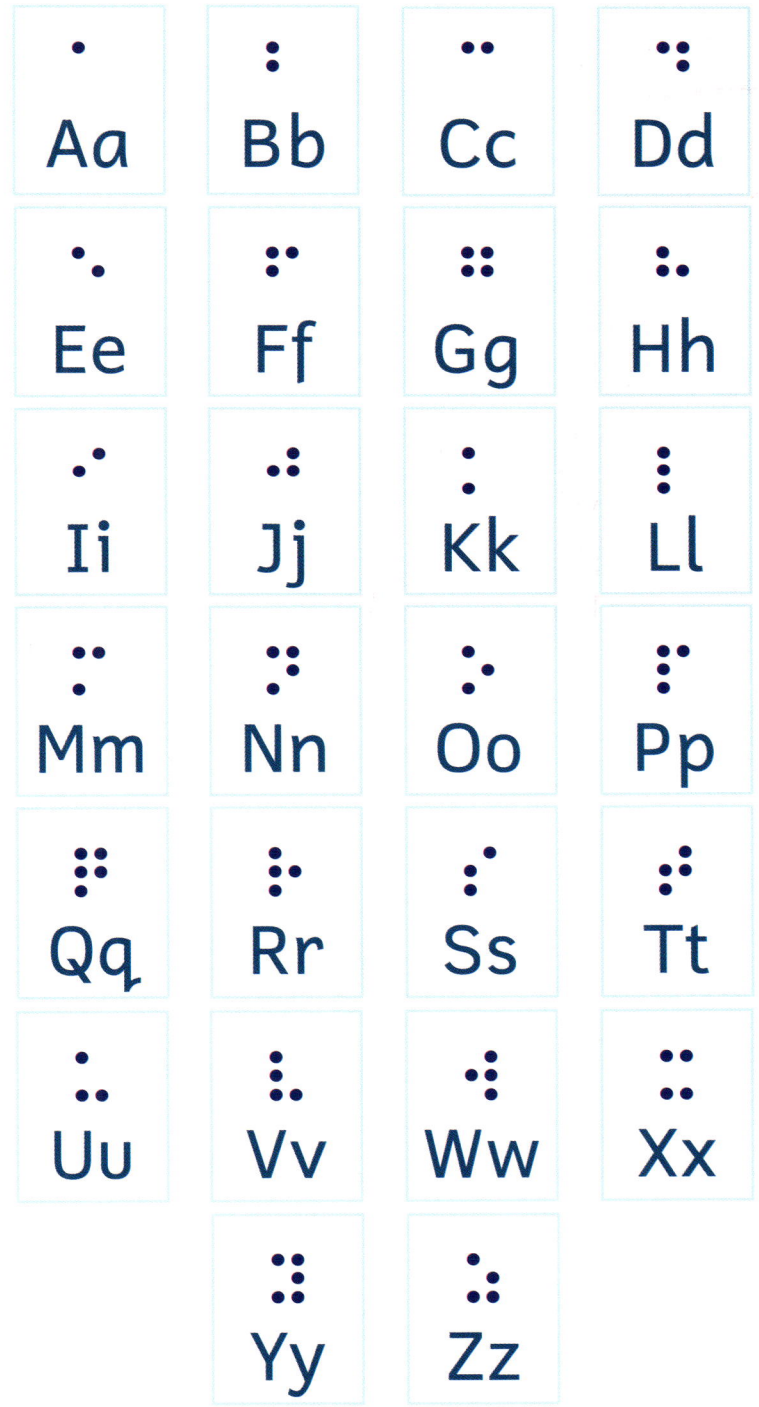

Chapter 1
Meeting Mr. Foster

Michael loves music. Today is his first piano lesson.

"Hello, Michael! Are you ready to make some music?" Mr. Foster asks.

Mr. Foster is a kind man who loves teaching piano. He has a warm smile and a gentle voice.

"I can't wait!" Michael replies.

Michael is blind, so he can't read sheet music. Mr. Foster explains that he will learn the notes by listening to them first. Then he will find them on the piano.

"Let's get started. Take a seat," Mr. Foster says, tapping the piano bench.

Mr. Foster plays a note and says its name.

Then, he places his hand over Michael's and guides Michael's fingers to the key.

Michael feels the key under his fingers. He memorizes its position.

"Now, you try finding that note," Mr. Foster says.

Michael listens carefully. Then, he presses a key. It's not quite right. He tries again and again until he finds the right note.

"Great job, Michael!" Mr. Foster says.

They keep playing. They laugh at mistakes. They have fun. Michael enjoys every moment.

Chapter 2
Wrong Notes

Michael practices piano every day. But learning to play piano is not easy.

Each time Michael makes a mistake, he starts the song over from the beginning.

Over time, Michael gets better. His fingers move confidently across the keys. He starts to master some of his favorite songs.

One day at lessons, Mr. Foster has exciting news for Michael.

"There's a recital coming up. Would you like to perform in it?" he asks.

"I'd love to!" Michael exclaims.

Michael and Mr. Foster pick a song. Michael works on it, but it's hard. He keeps hitting a wrong note in the same spot.

Frustrated, he starts over again and again.

"Why can't I do it?" Michael asks, feeling upset.

"It's okay, Michael," Mr. Foster says. "Everyone makes mistakes, especially when learning something new. Let's break it down."

Mr. Foster plays the notes slowly. Michael listens carefully. Then, he finds the notes on the piano.

They repeat this process until Michael feels more confident.

"Remember, every mistake is a step toward getting better," Mr. Foster says. "Just keep practicing."

Chapter 3
The Recital

The day of the recital arrives. Michael is excited. His family is there to support him.

When it's his turn, Michael takes a deep breath. He walks onto the stage and leans his cane on the side of the piano.

Michael sits down and smiles. He loves to perform, and he really loves a crowd. He places his fingers on the keys and begins to play.

Michael plays the song with joy. He plays it almost perfectly. As he hits the last note, the room fills with cheers.

"You are so good!" his sister says, hugging him tightly.

"Thanks, Karissa. I couldn't have done it without Mr. Foster," Michael replies.

Michael's mom beams with pride. "All your hard work really paid off."

"I want to play piano just like you" his brother says.

"I can help you, Mitchell," Michael says. "With practice, you can do anything!"

"You sure can," his mom agrees. "How would you like to join the after-school music program?"

So that's where Michael went the next Monday and lots of Mondays after that.

He met new friends and started singing. Michael's music dreams were just starting.

More About Michael

This story is based on the life of the author's oldest son, Michael. He started taking piano lessons with Mr. Foster in first grade. His favorite part of learning piano was performing at recitals.

In sixth grade, Michael joined an after-school club where he met friends and formed a band. Michael played keyboard and sang. The band performed together through high school.

Michael and his real-life piano teacher, Mr. Foster.

Michael still enjoys filling the family's home with piano music. His brother, Mitchell, learned to play guitar, and they often play together.

How Kim Creates

At 6 years old, Kim Crothers was diagnosed with a rare eye disease. Autosomal Dominant Optic Atrophy (ADOA) causes her to have low vision and color blindness.

A love of art led Kim to pursue her degree in graphic design at Mississippi State University. This set up her career as a freelance illustrator, artist, and graphic designer.

When Kim isn't drawing, she spends time with her husband, three kids, three dogs, and her parents in Madison, Mississippi.

How do you draw with limited vision?

When I'm drawing on paper, I use a thick black marker. I am able to see bold lines better than thin lines. I also make my drawings large so they are easier for me to see.

My digital tablet has accessibility tools that make it easier for me to draw. The tools allow me to zoom in on images.

I wear bioptic glasses too. The glasses have mini telescopes on the lenses. They make images larger so it's easier for me to see when I'm drawing.

Kim wearing bioptic glasses.

Think and Share

1. Michael makes mistakes and keeps trying. Why is it important to make mistakes?

2. Michael likes to perform and is excited about the recital. How do you feel about performing?

3. Because Michael can't see, Mr. Foster uses different methods to help him learn. Look back in the story and find examples.

About the Author

Kristin Smedley is a TEDx speaker, award-winning author, trailblazer for the disability community, and mother of three children, two of whom were born blind.

Kristin is a cofounder and CEO of the only patient organization in the world for people living with the rare eye disease CRB1 LCA/RP, which caused her two sons' blindness. She also cofounded Thriving Blind Academy.

Kristin lives in Pennsylvania, where she works endlessly to teach others how to move past their fears and obstacles to achieve their dreams.